Flatfoot Fox

and the Case of the Nosy Otter

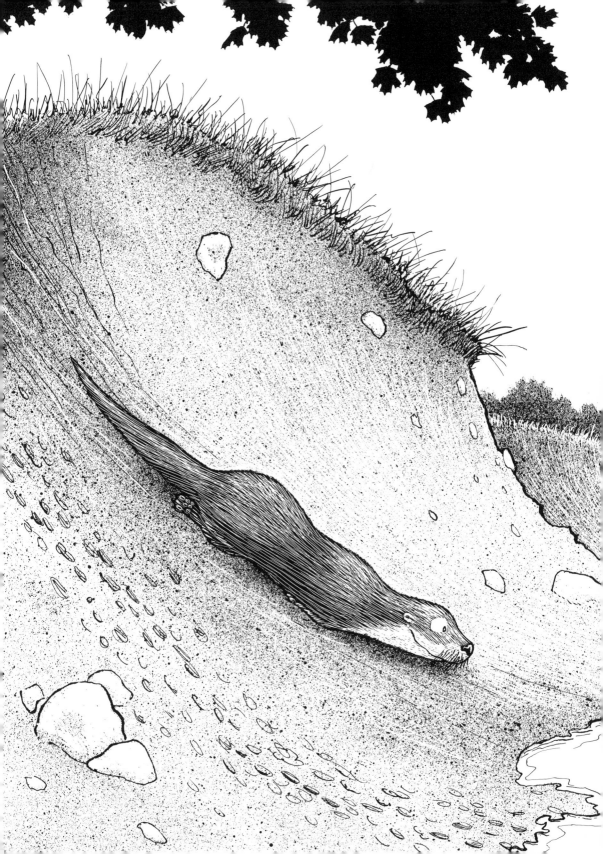

Flatfoot Fox

and the Case of the Nosy Otter

ETH CLIFFORD

Illustrated by Brian Lies

Houghton Mifflin Company

Boston 1992

For my very dear Charlotte
and each and every one
in my beautiful English family

—E.C.

For Elaine
—B.L.

Library of Congress Cataloging-in-Publication Data

Clifford, Eth.
  Flatfoot Fox and the case of the Nosy Otter / by Eth Clifford ;
illustrated by Brian Lies.
      p. cm.
  Summary: Mrs. Chatterbox Otter asks Flatfoot Fox to find her
missing son.
  ISBN 0-395-60289-0
  [1. Mystery and detective stories. 2. Foxes—Fiction.
3. Animals—Fiction.] I. Lies, Brian, ill. II. Title.
PZ7.C62214Fo 1992   91-26930
[Fic]—dc20   CIP
                          AC

Printed in the United States of America

HOR   10 9 8 7 6 5 4 3 2 1

Contents

1.   Mrs. Chatterbox Otter   7

2.   Crabby Crow   15

3.   Terribly Worried Woodchuck   21

4.   Lame-Brain Swan   29

5.   Motherly Mouse   35

6.   Mysteries Wanted   43

1.
Mrs. Chatterbox Otter

Knock! Knock!

Someone was knocking at Flatfoot Fox's door.

"Someone is knocking at the door," said Secretary Bird.

"I know that," said Flatfoot Fox. "I am the smartest detective in the whole world. I know when someone is knocking at my door."

"Who is there?" called Secretary Bird.

The door opened.

In came Mrs. Chatterbox Otter.

"Which one of you is the smartest detective in the whole world?" she asked.

"I am," Flatfoot Fox told her. "Who are you? And why do you need a detective?"

"I am Mrs. Chatterbox Otter. I need a detective because I am desperate."

"Desperate?" Secretary Bird repeated.

"Desperate," Flatfoot Fox said. He looked pleased. He always looked pleased when he was about to start on a new case.

Mrs. Chatterbox Otter nodded. "Desperate and furious! Furious and miserable! Miserable and scared!"

She cried and sniffed, and sniffed and cried.

"Someone has kidnapped my poor baby. He's gone, and I can't find him anywhere. My poor Nosy. He's been kidnapped. I want you to find the kidnapper. I want the monster who kidnapped Nosy to go to jail forever."

Secretary Bird was surprised.

"Monster?" he asked Flatfoot Fox. "I didn't know we had monsters around here."

Secretary Bird had never seen a monster. But he was afraid of them just the same.

"There are no monsters around here," Flatfoot Fox told him. "But monster is a good word for anyone who is a kidnapper."

He turned to Mrs. Chatterbox Otter.

"Where was your baby the last time you saw him?" he asked.

"Swimming in the river. No. Wait. He was going up and down the mud slide. It's such fun. Have you ever tried a mud slide?"

Flatfoot Fox shook his head.

Secretary Bird made a face.

Mrs. Chatterbox Otter didn't wait for an answer. She said, "I only turned my back on Nosy a minute to talk to Crabby Crow. Well, not to talk. I just wanted to ask him something. When I turned back, my darling Nosy Otter was gone. Stolen almost from my arms, you might say. Kidnapped."

Flatfoot Fox looked at Secretary Bird. Secretary Bird looked at Flatfoot Fox.

"Do you think she ever stops talking?" whispered Secretary Bird.

Flatfoot Fox whispered back, "Never." He stared at Mrs. Chatterbox Otter, who was still talking, and shouted, "STOP!"

Mrs. Chatterbox Otter's mouth stayed wide open.

Secretary Bird thought he could see lots of words left over in her mouth.

"I want you to take me to the place where you last saw little Nosy," said Flatfoot Fox. "I'm sure I can pick up the trail of the kidnapper."

"Why do you call him Nosy?" Secretary Bird wanted to know.

Mrs. Chatterbox Otter was happy to start talking again.

"Don't you know?" she asked. "Otters are very curious. Baby otters are especially curious. Nosy is curious about everything. He . . ."

She was still talking as she led the way through the door. Next came Secretary Bird, then Flatfoot Fox.

Mrs. Chatterbox Otter chattered.

FLATFOOT
FOX
THE SMARTES
DETECTIVE
IN THE
WHOLE
WORLD

OUT ON
A CASE
BACK
SOMETIME

Secretary Bird held his head high so the words wouldn't reach him.

Flatfoot Fox wore earmuffs left over from another case.

2.
Crabby Crow

"Here we are," said Mrs. Chatterbox Otter at last. "Now there's the river we swim in. And here's the mud slide. Are you sure you don't want to try it? Not even once?"

"NO!" said Secretary Bird.

"Not ever," said Flatfoot Fox.

"Oh, my poor little Nosy. He was so happy on that slide." Mrs. Chatterbox Otter sniffed and cried. "My darling little Nosy. So beautiful! So clever. So . . ."

"Babble, babble, babble," said an angry voice. It belonged to Crabby Crow, who sat on a branch just above them.

"Babble all day long. That one can talk till your ears fall off."

Flatfoot Fox didn't listen to Mrs. Chatterbox Otter. He didn't listen to Crabby Crow. He stared at the ground.

"What are you looking for?" Secretary Bird whispered. "What do you see?"

"Footprints," said Flatfoot Fox. "Lots of them."

"Are they monster footprints?" Secretary Bird looked here, there, and everywhere. He was scared.

"No. These are not monster footprints."

"Then whose footprints are they?" Secretary Bird asked.

"Everyone comes to the river," Flatfoot Fox explained. "It is a busy place." He pointed at the ground. "Now these footprints were made by little Nosy Otter."

He looked up at Crabby Crow. Then he asked, "Would you like to be my air scout?"

"Air scout? What do I have to do?" asked Crabby Crow.

"You can see things up high I can't see down here. You might spot Nosy Otter and his kidnapper."

"All right," Crabby Crow agreed. "I'll do it. But only if I get a promise from Mrs. Chatterbox Otter."

"What promise?" asked Mrs. Chatterbox Otter. "I think making a promise is very important. I think you have to be sure you can keep a promise. I think . . ."

Crabby Crow croaked in his crabbiest voice,
"There she goes again. I'll be your air scout," he
told Flatfoot Fox, "if she promises not to talk for
one whole day."

"Stop talking? For one whole day?" Mrs. Chatterbox Otter cried.

"One whole day. And night," Crabby Crow said.
"Not a single word for twenty-four hours."

18

"I'll explode if I can't talk," she cried.

Crabby Crow flapped his wings. "Yes or no? Do I go or stay?"

"Go. Please. Please go," she told him. So Crabby Crow flew off to be a scout.

"I'm going to follow the trail of these footprints," Flatfoot Fox told her. "You wait here in case the kidnapper returns little Nosy."

Mrs. Chatterbox Otter opened her mouth.

"SHHHH!" Secretary Bird warned. "Remember. No talking for twenty-four hours."

Secretary Bird and Flatfoot Fox left her to follow the trail.

"Do you think she can keep quiet for a whole day and night?" asked Secretary Bird.

"Maybe she'll find out how wonderful silence can be," Flatfoot Fox said. "Now let's follow this trail quickly. There isn't a moment to lose."

3.
Terribly Worried Woodchuck

The footprints they followed zigged this way and zagged that way. Zig-zag. Zig-zag.

Flatfoot Fox stopped for a moment to study the ground. "Aha!" he said. "Now there are other foot-prints, too. They must belong to the kidnapper."

"His footprints zigzag, too. Did the kidnapper know he might be followed?" asked Secretary Bird. "Was he trying to throw us off his trail by zigging and zagging?"

"It seems that way," Flatfoot Fox answered. "But it is not easy to fool the smartest detective in the whole world."

"Can you tell who the kidnapper is from his foot-prints?" Secretary Bird wanted to know.

Before Flatfoot Fox could answer, a voice spoke from behind them.

"Who are you?" it demanded. "What do you want?"

They spun around.

"The kidnapper!" Secretary Bird shouted. "We've caught the kidnapper!"

"Kidnapper? I'm Terribly Worried Woodchuck. Why are you calling me a kidnapper?" he asked.

"We have just found your footprints next to the footprints of little Nosy Otter, who is *missing*." Flatfoot Fox gave Terribly Worried Woodchuck a suspicious look.

"You monster!" Secretary Bird screamed.

Terribly Worried Woodchuck looked over his shoulder. "Where?" he cried. He was scared.

"You're the monster. You kidnapped little Nosy Otter. The case is solved," Secretary Bird announced. "I have solved this case."

"Nothing is solved until I say so," Flatfoot Fox said.

"Don't be ridiculous," said Terribly Worried Woodchuck. "Why would I kidnap anybody? Don't I have enough problems?"

"What problems?" Flatfoot Fox wanted to know.

"How can you ask? Do you have to come up from your underground home every year to look for your shadow?"

"No," said Flatfoot Fox. "I don't have to look for my shadow. I always know where it is."

"I toss and turn in my sleep all winter," Terribly

Worried Woodchuck complained. "I worry whether I will see my shadow when I come out. If I do, there will be six more weeks of winter. Everyone will say it's my fault."

"That's so silly," Secretary Bird said. "You're just a woodchuck. Don't you know the groundhog is supposed to do that? That's why we have Groundhog Day."

Flatfoot Fox shook his head. "He's the groundhog. A groundhog is a woodchuck. A woodchuck is a groundhog."

"I hate being called a hog. It isn't dignified. I am a very dignified woodchuck," said Terribly Worried Woodchuck.

"What happens if you don't see your shadow?" asked Secretary Bird.

"Then spring comes early, of course. Then everyone likes me."

Flatfoot Fox was impatient.

"This doesn't help us find little Nosy Otter. And we still don't know whether you are the kidnapper. Don't forget that the footprints near yours were made by little Nosy Otter. Where have you hidden him?"

"He may have followed me. Otters are very curious, you know," said Terribly Worried Woodchuck.

"Curious about what?" asked Flatfoot Fox.

"Everything!"

"Do you mean you haven't seen him?" Secretary Bird asked.

"No. I haven't seen him. I don't want to see him. I have no time for curious baby otters."

"What do we do now?" asked Secretary Bird as he and Flatfoot Fox left.

"We'll keep on doing what we've been doing."

"You mean follow Nosy Otter's footprints?" Secretary Bird asked.

"Of course," Flatfoot Fox answered.

Behind them, they could hear Terribly Worried Woodchuck wail, "Why me? Why my shadow? It isn't fair."

4.
Lame-Brain Swan

"There's a pond up ahead," said Flatfoot Fox. "And Nosy Otter's footprints lead right to it."

"But there are other footprints, too," Secretary Bird pointed out. "They must belong to the kidnapper." He was very proud. He thought, I'm a good detective, too. Maybe I can be the smartest detective in the whole world someday.

Just then Crabby Crow flew down and landed on a branch.

"There's a house in a meadow —" he began.

"Not now," said Secretary Bird. "Can't you see we're hot on the trail of the kidnapper? We're sure we'll find him at the pond."

"A house would be a good hiding place," Crabby Crow said.

But Flatfoot Fox didn't listen. Secretary Bird didn't listen. They hurried to the pond. The footprints ended at the edge of the water, but there was no sign of Nosy Otter or anyone else, except for a swan. He was staring at his reflection in the water.

"How handsome I am," he said. "Is there anyone in the world as handsome as I am?"

"That's Lame-Brain Swan," Crabby Crow explained. "You won't learn anything from him. He never makes any sense at all. Of course," he went on, "someone that handsome doesn't have to make sense."

Lame-Brain Swan looked up and saw them.

"I want to ask you a question," said Flatfoot Fox as soon as Lame-Brain came close.

"A penny saved is a penny earned," said Lame-Brain Swan.

"What?" Flatfoot Fox asked in surprise.

"An apple a day keeps the doctor away," Lame-Brain went on.

Secretary Bird was puzzled. "Which doctor?"

"Witches fly only at night" was Lame-Brain's answer.

Flatfoot Fox was angry. "Stop that nonsense this minute," he shouted. "Nosy Otter was here. These are his footprints. There are other footprints, too. Who came here with Nosy Otter?"

"A search is not over until it's over," said Lame-Brain. He drifted away slowly.

"Let's circle the pond," Flatfoot Fox said. "Maybe we will pick up Nosy Otter's footprints again."

"I say let's go to the house," said Crabby Crow. "I'll fly ahead and keep watch."

Flatfoot Fox didn't answer. He studied the ground around the pond. At last he cried, "Aha! I knew it. Here are more of Nosy Otter's footprints."

"What about these other footprints next to his?" Secretary Bird asked. "They look very small."

"We'll soon find out whose they are. Let's see where they lead us," said Flatfoot Fox.

5.
Motherly Mouse

"Crabby Crow was right," said Secretary Bird. "The footprints have led us right to the house."

"I knew they would," said Flatfoot Fox. "But I didn't guess. I made sure. That's why I'm the smartest detective in the whole world."

"No one is home," Crabby Crow called to them as they came closer. "I haven't seen Nosy Otter. I haven't seen anybody."

Flatfoot Fox smiled. "There is someone in the house. That someone is peeking out at us from behind the curtain. Follow me."

Crabby Crow waited on a branch while Flatfoot Fox and Secretary Bird went up to the front door.

"Open up!" Flatfoot Fox shouted. He banged on

the door. "I know you're in there."

The door opened at once.

"Who are you?" asked Secretary Bird.

"I'm Motherly Mouse. How nice of you to come for tea. You're just in time. No, no, no!" she scolded. "First wipe your feet on the mat. I don't allow muddy, dirty feet in my house. There. That's better."

Motherly Mouse beamed at them after they wiped their feet on the mat.

When they stepped inside, she said, "Now go and wash this minute. No one sits at my table without washing."

"Hi!" called a cheery voice.

Secretary Bird and Flatfoot Fox stared.

"Are you hungry? I'm starved. When do we eat?"

"You're Nosy Otter," said Flatfoot Fox.

"I'm hungry Nosy Otter," said Nosy Otter. He shouted again, "When do we eat?"

"Manners," said Motherly Mouse. "Manners,

manners. We do not shout at the table. We talk nicely, and say please and thank you."

She made Flatfoot Fox and Secretary Bird sit down at the table. Then she tied bibs on them. "No sloppy eaters wanted here. Isn't that right, son?" she asked Nosy Otter.

"Son?" asked Flatfoot Fox.

"I found this poor lost baby . . ."

"I wasn't lost," said Nosy Otter. "I knew where I was all the time."

"But your mother didn't know," Flatfoot Fox scolded. "She thought you were kidnapped."

Nosy Otter was surprised. "She did? I'm sorry. I just wanted to see the world. The world is a very interesting place."

"I took him in," said Motherly Mouse. "This place has always been so lonely. But now I have a son. He was lost and I found him. Finders, keepers. Everyone knows that. Here, son," she said in a gentle voice. "Have some more cookies."

"I can't have more because I haven't had any yet," Nosy Otter said.

38

Flatfoot Fox stood up. "Finders are not keepers. A son belongs to his mother. Come along," he told Nosy Otter. "I'm taking you home."

"Do come and see me sometime," Motherly Mouse called after Nosy Otter as they all left.

Secretary Bird walked in front of Nosy Otter. Flatfoot Fox walked behind him. Crabby Crow flew overhead.

Nosy Otter would not be allowed to go exploring again.

6.
Mysteries Wanted

"Well," said Secretary Bird, "I'm glad the case of the nosy otter is over. Mrs. Chatterbox Otter was so happy, she almost forgot to talk."

"Yes," Flatfoot Fox agreed. "I am happy we finally found her son."

"Why are otters so curious?" Secretary Bird wanted to know.

"It's just the way they are. They can't help it. Aren't you ever curious?" asked Flatfoot Fox.

Secretary Bird was puzzled. "Curious about what?"

"About anything."

Secretary Bird thought and thought. "No. I am never curious," he answered. "I don't have a curious bone in my body."

Flatfoot Fox laughed. "Now *that's* curious."

Secretary Bird laughed, too. After a while he said, "I guess all's well that ends well."

"Don't say that," Flatfoot Fox ordered. "You sounded just like Lame-Brain Swan."

Secretary Bird was surprised. "But isn't all well that ends well?"

"Never mind," Flatfoot Fox told him.

Both were quiet for a long time. Flatfoot Fox kept watching the door. Finally he sighed. "I wish someone would knock."

"Who?" asked Secretary Bird.

"Anyone at all. There must be somebody who needs my help. How can I be the smartest detective in the whole world if I don't have a mystery to solve?"

Secretary Bird said, "We could put a sign up outside the door. MYSTERIES WANTED."

"That would not be dignified," Flatfoot Fox said.

They waited and waited. No one knocked. No one opened the door.

44

"I think I will go for a walk," Flatfoot Fox said.

"Shall I come with you?"

"No. You stay here."

Flatfoot Fox reached out to open the door. It was pulled open so hard from the other side he almost fell over.

But he wasn't angry.

He smiled.

His next case had just arrived.